Ladybird books are widely available, but in case of
difficulty may be ordered by post or telephone from:

Ladybird Books – Cash Sales Department
Littlegate Road Paignton Devon TQ3 3BE
Telephone 01803 554761

A catalogue record for this book is available
from the British Library

Published by Ladybird Books Ltd Loughborough Leicestershire UK
LADYBIRD and the device of a Ladybird are trademarks of Ladybird Books Ltd

Britt Allcroft's Magic Adventures of Mumfie
Created by Britt Allcroft from the works of Katharine Tozer
Written by Britt Allcroft and John Kane
Song lyrics by John Kane
© Britt Allcroft (Mumfie) Ltd MCMXCV
All rights worldwide Britt Allcroft (Mumfie) Ltd
MUMFIE is a trademark of Britt Allcroft (Mumfie) Ltd
The BRITT ALLCROFT logo is a trademark of The Britt Allcroft Group Ltd

Britt Allcroft's
Magic Adventures of

Mumfie™

A Treasure Beyond Price

Ladybird

The story so far…

Mumfie, the special little elephant, had set off to look for an exciting adventure.

With the help of a friendly whale he had found an enchanted island, ruled by the Queen of Night. But the  Queen's wicked Secretary had stolen her magic and turned the island into a prison.

Mumfie, with his friends, Scarecrow, Pinkey and Napoleon, was determined to come to the Queen's rescue and free Pinkey's mother, who was imprisoned on the island.

Mumfie knew the only
way to help the Queen
and Pinkey's mother
was to protect the Queen's
magic jewel and
umbrella from the
wicked Secretary and
find the magic cloak of
dreams.

Now, with Whale, Scarecrow,
Pinkey and Napoleon, Mumfie
watched as storm clouds gathered over
the mysterious and enchanted island…

Mumfie and his friends shivered. "I fear the Secretary must know we have the Queen's jewel," said Napoleon. "His anger will soon destroy the island. Her Majesty is in *great* danger."

"So is Pinkey's mother," whispered Mumfie. "We must get the Queen's jewel back to Her Majesty! We'll have to fly!"

Pinkey climbed onto Napoleon's back. Napoleon stretched his wings and took off.

Mumfie looked at Scarecrow. "We'll have to use the Queen's umbrella and hope its magic works again," he said.

And luckily it did! Mumfie and Scarecrow were gently lifted into the air and began floating towards the island.

Meanwhile, the wicked Secretary was in the Queen of Night's palace. He knew that Mumfie and his friends were coming…

"The little elephant must be destroyed and then the jewel will be *mine*," he hissed.

He flung open a window and flew off on the night wind. The black cat, clinging to his shoulder, knew she must do whatever she could to save Mumfie and his friends.

Soon, the Secretary loomed above Mumfie and Scarecrow as they clung on tightly to the Queen's umbrella.

"Jump," the cat whispered to Mumfie. "My magic will keep you safe." Mumfie decided to trust the black cat and let go of the umbrella.

"Mumfie!" cried Scarecrow, who was too afraid to do the same, "come back!"

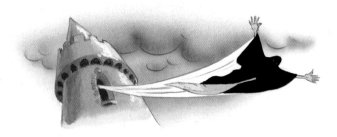

Down, down, down Mumfie fell.

At last, when Mumfie's head had stopped spinning, he realised he had landed in a dewy meadow. To his great relief, the Queen's jewel was still safely tucked in his pocket.

But there in the distance was Davy Jones, the pirate captain. He was washing the tattoos off his arm. Mumfie was amazed.

"These aren't *real* tattoos as I was never a *real* pirate," Davy Jones explained, sadly. "I was just lonely and bored, so I got up to mischief."

"That's no excuse," said Mumfie, firmly. "There's a lot of other things you could have done. You just have to use your imagination."

"I'm imagining that I'm back at sea," said Davy Jones. "But who would ever trust me or hire me to go sailing again with my reputation?"

"I would!" cried Mumfie, and handed Davy Jones the penny he'd been carrying in his pocket since he left home. "Take this lucky penny and report for duty immediately. You can be deck steward on the Good Ship Whale!"

"But I chased Whale and tied him up not so long ago," said Davy Jones. "He'd never forgive me for that."

"Whale has got an awfully big heart," replied Mumfie. "Why don't you go and ask him?" So Davy Jones, much encouraged, saluted smartly and set off towards the sea.

But Mumfie still had company. The black cat had appeared mysteriously again and was sitting in a tree.

"I'm here to help you," she purred. "I've been trying to do that ever since we met at the crossroads. I'm afraid the Secretary caught Napoleon but your friends Scarecrow and Pinkey escaped. They're hiding in the palace. Come on, I'll take you there."

All at once, a huge gust of wind swept Mumfie and the cat high into the air and towards the palace. "Don't dawdle!" the black cat cried. "It's way past my teatime!"

In the palace, Mumfie and the black cat crept past the Secretary's office. But just then Bristle, the Secretary's prison guard, appeared.

"Well, if it isn't the horrible little elephant!" he said, nastily. "You're just in time. The Secretary wants to meet you." And Bristle knocked on the Secretary's door.

"Quickly! Give me the Queen's jewel," the cat whispered to Mumfie. So, when Bristle was looking the other way, Mumfie reluctantly did so.

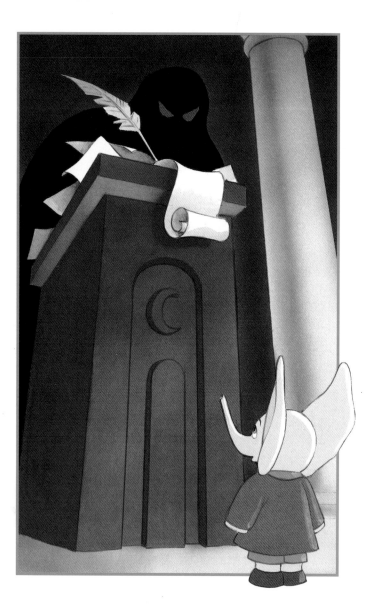

Then, the door to the Secretary's office opened and there stood the wicked Secretary.

"Now!" he snarled. "Where is the jewel?"

"It must be awfully tiring being so angry all the time," said Mumfie, brightly. "Don't you ever smile?"

This made the Secretary even more angry. "Lock him in a cell!" he hissed at Bristle. "Give him no food or water until he tells us where the jewel is. That'll make him change his tune."

"I know lots of tunes," said Mumfie, and he started to whistle a particularly cheery one.

The Secretary took hold of Mumfie's trunk and squeezed. But Mumfie continued to whistle even though his eyes were watering. Then, still whistling, Mumfie was led away and Bristle locked him up all alone in a cold cell.

The hours passed slowly and Mumfie grew colder and colder.

At last, he heard a key in the lock. The door opened and someone tall and thin with sticking out hair stood in the doorway.

"Scarecrow!" cried Mumfie, running into his arms. Scarecrow lifted up his little friend and hugged him tightly.

At that very moment, Pinkey flew round the corner of the cell.

"I've found Napoleon!" she said. "This way – quickly!"

Mumfie and Scarecrow followed Pinkey to the strangest room they had ever seen. It was filled with filing cabinets and piles and piles of paper – but there was no sign of Napoleon!

In the distance, they heard someone approaching – it was Bristle. Mumfie and Scarecrow pushed one of the cabinets over to block the doorway. A drawer in the cabinet popped open, and there was – Napoleon!

Everyone was so surprised that they didn't notice the black cat suddenly appear again. She crept up to Mumfie and put the Queen's jewel back into his pocket.

As Bristle's footsteps got closer, the friends hurried towards the only window to escape – but it wouldn't open.

"We'll have to break it," said Scarecrow, as he grabbed a heavy, glass paperweight. "Everyone – stand back!" He put the paperweight in his hat and swung it at the window. The window shattered into hundreds of pieces.

The paperweight broke too! There was something inside it. Scarecrow picked it up. It was a small, silver thimble.

"And what's inside this thimble?" whispered Scarecrow. "It's swirling and *very* mysterious."

"It's the Queen of Night's magic cloak!" cried Napoleon. "You've found it!"

Scarecrow quickly slipped the thimble into one of his pockets, just as Bristle came bursting into the room.

The friends had to get away – fast!

Mumfie and Scarecrow scrambled onto Napoleon's back. Then Napoleon and Pinkey spread their wings and flew out of the window, side by side.

As they raced through the air, Mumfie turned round and saw a large, black shadow following them.

"Give *me* the thimble!" hissed the Secretary.

"We've got to take evasive action!" called Napoleon. "Hang on tight!"

Napoleon began to twist and turn in the air to try and throw the Secretary off their trail. Then, hiding in a dark cloud, he stayed very still, until it was safe to start moving again. The Secretary was nowhere to be seen – neither was Pinkey!

"I hope Pinkey's all right," said Mumfie, as Napoleon came down to land in the Queen of Night's garden.

"You find Her Majesty," Napoleon panted, "and I'll search for Pinkey." And off he flew.

Mumfie and Scarecrow found the Queen in her garden, looking very sad.

"We think this thimble may hold your magic cloak of dreams, Your Majesty," said Scarecrow, holding the thimble out towards the Queen. But just as he did so, the wicked Secretary stepped out of the shadows and snatched the thimble.

The very next moment, there was a blur of pink in the air and the thimble was gone.

"It's Pinkey!" cried Mumfie, as their little friend dropped the thimble into the Queen's waiting hands.

The Queen quickly blew into the thimble and her magic cloak rose out of it in a cloud of sparkling mist full of wonderful colours and shapes.

Then, it wrapped itself around the Secretary like a snake until he was completely out of sight.

When the cloak had disappeared, the Secretary had turned into a large, empty, stone inkwell.

"Gosh, that really is a magic cloak," said Mumfie.

"Now, will you set my mother free, please?" Pinkey asked the Queen.

"Free them all!" said the Queen, and at her command, the cloak of dreams swirled into the air again and swept off towards the palace dungeons.

All the prison doors sprang open and the first prisoner set free was Pinkey's mother!

The next day, when laughter and music had returned to the island, the Queen held a special party in her garden.

Even Bristle was looking happy. "I've seen the error of my ways," he declared. "The only orders I'll follow now are Her Majesty's."

The Queen presented Mumfie, Scarecrow and Pinkey with silver medals in the shape of thimbles.

"You have been trusting, kind and courageous," she said, "and you have brought peace and happiness back to this island."

"I'm still very sorry I lost your jewel, Your Majesty," said Mumfie.

"Why don't you look in your pocket?" suggested the Queen.

And to his amazement, Mumfie saw that the jewel was there!

"You may keep it," said the Queen, kindly.

"But," gasped Mumfie, "it's a treasure beyond price!"

"So it is, for those who receive it," replied the Queen. "You should get ready to go home now, Mumfie."

And so Mumfie and Scarecrow said goodbye to their good friends and set off for home.

As they walked along the beach, they looked out to sea.

"There's Whale!" cried Scarecrow, "but who's that with him?"

"I know who it is," laughed Mumfie. "It's Davy Jones and he's polishing the portholes as bright as a new penny. Whale is making his wish come true."

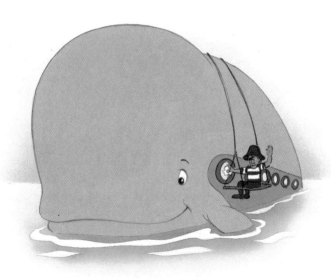

Later, as Mumfie and Scarecrow were walking down the lane where their adventure had first begun, they came across the little bird sitting in the bare tree.

"Did you bring something back?" asked the bird.

"Yes I did," said Mumfie. "I brought the tree a present." He took out the Queen's jewel and hung it on the tree. Then he gasped, for suddenly the tree was covered with beautiful leaves and flowers.

"Oh, how lovely!" said Mumfie.

Moments later, they heard voices. "Mumfie! Scarecrow! We're here!"

Turning round, they saw their friends, Mr and Mrs Admiral, standing at the door of Mumfie's cottage.

"How lucky I am to have so many wonderful friends," Mumfie said to himself. "Scarecrow," he said out loud, "will you keep me company always? We can have lots more adventures."

"Of course I will," said Scarecrow. And smiling happily, he and Mumfie went indoors.

Home, everybody has a place they think of.
Home, though it may be long ago.
Roam all around the world that's
*   full of strangers*
There's always one place you'll know.

There, waiting for you in the open doorway.
There, like a dear familiar song.
Stare into yesterday to find that someone
You've been missing so long.

Someone with a loving heart that beats
  like your heart.
Someone with a smile that makes
  your smile grow wider.
Someone who can make a place you've
  never been to feel like home.
And that someone is you!

And what happens next? Well, what do you think?